PATTY AND THE SHADOWS

HI, THERE – I'm Patty Mills.

I play basketball in the NBA, and I've represented Australia at the Olympics three times. That's these days. Growing up, I was a sports-loving kid just like you. And that's why I'm excited about my new series of kids' books, Game Day!

Patty, the main character, loves playing every sport he can – especially basketball. He learns many important skills and values through sports, dancing, and of course, at school. He also has a whole lot of fun with his friends, but when it comes to game day, he always makes sure he's ready to perform.

I think you're going to love taking this journey with Patty. Have fun reading the series, don't miss the glossary in the back of every book, and I hope to see you on the basketball court one day!

THE GAME DAY! SERIES

BOOK 1 *Patty Hits the Court*

BOOK 2 *Patty and the Shadows*

BOOK 3 *Patty Takes Charge*

First American Edition 2020
Kane Miller, A Division of EDC Publishing

Text copyright © Patty Mills and Jared Thomas 2017
Illustrations copyright © Nahum Ziersch 2017
First published in Australia in 2017 by Allen & Unwin.
Cover design by Ruth Grüner and Nahum Ziersch.
Text design and typesetting by Ruth Grüner.
Cover illustration by Nahum Ziersch.

For information contact:
Kane Miller, A Division of EDC Publishing
PO Box 470663
Tulsa, OK 74147-0663
www.kanemiller.com
www.edcpub.com
www.usbornebooksandmore.com

Library of Congress Control Number: 2019940425

Printed and bound in the United States of America

1 2 3 4 5 6 7 8 9 10

ISBN: 978-1-68464-023-2

BOOK 2
PATTY MILLS
WITH JARED THOMAS

ILLUSTRATIONS BY NAHUM ZIERSCH

A DIVISION OF EDC PUBLISHING

CHAPTER 1

"SHOOT, PATTY, SHOOT," Josie called out as I caught the ball under the basket.

I shot an easy basket and then Tiago said, "I've had enough, we've been playing for hours."

"Come on, Tiago," Manu protested. "There's still daylight, let's keep playing."

Josie and I followed Tiago to the side of the court and slumped onto the grass.

"I wish the holidays didn't have to end," I complained, looking up at the clouds.

"Me too," Tiago said.

"At least you weren't sick for half the holidays, like me!"

"Well, at least you got to miss the last week of school!" Boris said.

"Yeah, stuck in bed the whole time," I reminded my friends. Although I'd had a high fever, I still remembered how frustrated I'd felt. I could see the basketball hoop on our garage outside my bedroom window, but I couldn't practice! Since I'd recovered I'd more than made up for lost time, and was either making layups at home or at the courts with my friends every day. I could tell my skills had improved. I was determined that my team would get further than the semifinals this year.

I picked up the ball again and headed back out onto the court.

"Gee, Patty, looks like you've really been working on your shot," Boris said when I made a layup. "Based on my calculations, you're a 50 percent better shooter than you were last season!"

I rolled my eyes at Boris, but I was pleased he'd noticed. "I'm going to play for Australia in the Olympics one day," I said. "Against you lot!" And I passed the ball to Boris. Boris was from France, Tiago was from Brazil and Manu was from Argentina, and one day they would all return to their home countries.

"Come on, let's play some more," I said. "Or at least go for a ride. I want to make the most of what's left of the holidays."

Josie's face was red and covered in sweat. "I need to refuel," she said. "Want to go to the milk bar?"

It was the best idea we'd heard all day.

WE RAN OUT of the milk bar to a picnic table in the park across the street. Josie ripped open the huge bag of mixed lollies we'd pooled our money to buy, and spread it on the table for us all to share.

Manu dove on the pile with both hands.

Tyson appeared down the street, riding his BMX. He pulled up at our table and grabbed a handful of lollies. "G'day, goody-goodies," he said.

"Where are you going?" I asked.

"Heading to the skate park," he said, grinning

at me before stuffing his mouth. "I've just been practicing my four hundred meters."

The last time we raced at athletics Tyson had only just beaten me. "You need all the practice you can get," I told him.

"Well, you'll get the chance to see me in action tonight, won't you, Patty?" He took some more lollies and rode off.

"Why does he always have to be like that?" Tiago asked, picking out the strawberries-and-creams.

It was our first athletics training for the new term that night. I wondered if Tyson really had been practicing. I didn't want him to thrash me; I'd been gaining ground on him before the end of last year.

CHAPTER

2

I SAT ON THE EDGE of my bed pulling on my shoes. I was starting to feel nervous about racing against Tyson. Sure, the gang and I had run around when we played basketball and cricket over the holidays, but it was ages since I'd practiced running seriously.

I looked up at my poster of Cathy Freeman. Mum would always ask me if I wanted to watch her famous four-hundred-meter race from the Sydney Olympics whenever I didn't feel like training. She knew it got me pumped.

I've watched the race hundreds of times, and the thing I love about it most is seeing Cathy's face afterwards. She doesn't look happy when she wins, but she does look really proud that she worked so hard.

As we stopped at the first set of traffic lights on the way to training, Dad asked, "What's wrong, Patty? You didn't get up to any trouble with your friends today, did you?"

"No," I told him, thinking about the mountain of lollies that we bought. "I'm just worried that Tyson might thrash me tonight."

"It's only practice," Dad said. But it was never

just practice when it came to Tyson and me competing against each other.

AT THE ATHLETICS PARK, Tyson, Boris, Manu, Tiago and I were doing flips onto the high jump mat when our coach marshaled us for the four hundred meters.

We started stretching for the race. The thing that I focused on before running the four hundred was my breathing. I wanted it to stay steady as I ran – I didn't want to be puffing and panting.

After a few minutes the coach called us up to our marks.

"Get ready, Shorty," Tyson teased.

He knew I was self-conscious about my height and that I hated being called Shorty. Now I *really* wanted to beat him.

When our coach, Cindy, fired the starting gun, I ran out of the blocks like I usually do, trying to stay close to the pack. I focused on getting my arms and legs pumping in a smooth rhythm along with my breathing. I had to pace myself – you can't win a race in the first few seconds.

By the middle of the first straight I realized that it was just Tyson and me, neck and neck.

I thought he might break ahead by the two-hundred-meter mark, but he stayed right there beside me. I needed to decide when to make my break. I told myself to keep up with him around the last bend, then go for it.

And as soon as we were into the home straight, I gave it everything I had.

It wasn't until I crossed the finish line and looked back that I realized I'd won. And it wasn't even close – I'd won the race by meters.

"That was a fluke, Shorty," Tyson said when he'd finally caught his breath. As he walked alongside me, I noticed that I'd grown. For the first time, I was almost as tall as Tyson.

CHAPTER 3

THE BEST THING about being back at school was having all my friends together to play basketball at recess and footy at lunchtime. There were always enough kids to play full teams, and our matches were serious. We kept score and nominated a referee who even used a whistle.

I had started playing tennis over the summer break and loved it, so I tried to play a couple of games of tennis with Manu during the week too.

Josie and I were excited to start training for our second season of basketball. We weren't beginners anymore; we'd learned skills and had even made the semifinals the year before. Now we were determined to play in our first grand final.

"G'day, Patty," Tyson said when I walked into the gym and picked up a ball. I was waiting for him to say something smart, but he stayed silent.

I took a shot from near the three-point line and it went in. It was the farthest from the basket I'd ever scored. I put my newfound strength down to my sudden growth – last year, shooting from the free-throw line had seemed almost impossible. I quietly pumped my fist, but then Tyson came over.

"If you can't hit three in a row, it's just a fluke," he said.

When my second shot bounced off the hoop, Tyson just laughed and walked away.

IN THE LESSON after basketball training my new teacher, Ms. Baker, told us, "We're going to be studying Aboriginal and Torres Strait Islander history and culture in the lead-up to Reconciliation Week and Mabo Day."

My face lit up when Ms. Baker said "Mabo Day" – it's named after my Grandad, Eddie Mabo, who went to the High Court of Australia and proved that the Murray Islands belong to Murray Island people.

"Not much to learn!" Tyson remarked. I felt the blood drain from my face.

"What do you mean, Tyson?" Ms. Baker asked.

"Well, what were Aborigines doing before

white people arrived? Just eating bugs and insects and things."

I looked at Josie, and I could tell that she was just as shocked and upset as I was. Tyson knew that Josie was Torres Strait Islander, and that my mum is Aboriginal and my dad is a Torres Strait Islander.

Ms. Baker flicked a glance at us to see if we were okay, then gave Tyson a serious look. "I think you'll find there's a lot to learn over the coming weeks, Tyson."

"Yeah, Aboriginal and Torres Strait Islanders have got some of the best foods going," I told him.

"Like lizards and witchetty grubs?" Tyson replied. "What would you know, Patty? You live in the city."

I was so angry, and Josie knew it. She leaned over to me and said, "Don't worry about it. He's just being a jerk."

Ms. Baker raised her voice over the laughing and talking. "Okay, Tyson, that's enough now." Then she moved on to the lesson about Aboriginal and Torres Strait Islander foods.

Ms. Baker explained how there are Aboriginal people on the mainland of Australia, and Torres Strait Island people of the Torres Strait. She showed us a map of Australia with hundreds of different-colored sections representing all the different Aboriginal language groups. Ms. Baker told the class how each group has its own culture. My mum's family are Kokatha people, and I knew that their culture and Dad's Torres Strait Islander culture were similar in some ways but also very different.

"The oldest tools in the world have been found in Australia," Ms. Baker said. "And Aboriginal people were the first to make bread, thousands of years before people from any other country."

"No way, really?" said Boris. It was something I hadn't known either. "That's impressive."

Then Ms. Baker listed a whole lot of foods that Aboriginal and Torres Strait Islander people eat that some of my classmates eat all the time. Some are served up in fancy restaurants.

Ms. Baker smiled when she said, "Seafood was commonly eaten by coastal Aboriginal people before European arrival in Australia, including some of my personal favorite foods, like snapper, salmon, whiting, oysters, prawns and crayfish."

"Ms. Baker, you're making me hungry!" Manu said.

"You're always hungry, Manu!" we all chorused.

Ms. Baker ended the class by saying, "Next time I'll talk about indigenous fruit and vegetables, some of which have far greater vitamin C content than even oranges."

Although Ms. Baker's class was amazing, I still felt sick in the stomach because of what Tyson had said. He might as well have said, "I think Aboriginal and Torres Strait Islander people are worthless."

CHAPTER

4

"DINNER'S READY," Mum called out, but I wasn't in the mood for eating. I just wanted to keep shooting hoops in the driveway.

After a while Dad poked his head out the front door and said, "You can give that a rest now and come and have dinner."

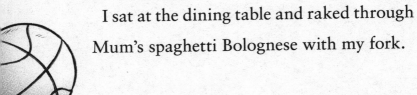

I sat at the dining table and raked through Mum's spaghetti Bolognese with my fork.

Mum said, "I thought you loved spaghetti?"

"I'd rather have some bush tucker."

Mum chuckled. "It's not that easy to get around here, Patty."

"It's great when your uncles send down things like turtle and dugong from the Torres Strait," Dad said, "but we need to save that for special occasions."

I sat there for a while longer, playing with my food. Eventually Mum put down her fork and asked, "What's wrong, Patty?"

"We're learning about Aboriginal and Torres Strait Islander things at school," I began.

"That's a good thing, though. You're not happy about it?"

"Tyson said something silly."

Dad sighed. "What did he say?"

"He said our people did nothing except eat bugs and grubs until his people came along."

I expected Dad and Mum to get angry, but they stayed calm.

"And is what Tyson said true?" Dad asked.

"I know it's not."

"Unfortunately, Patty, you're going to hear people say a lot of things about your people that are wrong. You need to hold in your heart what you know is true," Mum told me.

"Sometimes I wish I didn't need to worry about people saying silly things. I wish I could just be comfortable like I am in our dance group with other Torres Strait Islanders."

"Well," Dad said, "I have some news that might cheer you up."

"Really?" I asked. "What is it?"

"We've been talking to Uncle Noel about starting up a junior basketball team. It'll be for Aboriginal and Torres Strait Islander kids, and kids from diverse cultural backgrounds. Would you be interested? Josie's parents are asking her too. The team will be called the Shadows."

I didn't even need time to think about it. "Yes! I'd love to," I said. "Especially because I won't have to play with Tyson."

Mum gave me her serious look and said, "We don't want you to stop playing for the school team. And if what Tyson thinks is important to you, you're not going to change his mind by avoiding him."

"The important thing is not to avoid Tyson, you need to show him that Aboriginal and Torres Strait Islander kids are capable of just as much as anyone else," Dad said.

"But don't forget athletics and dancing too, Patty," Mum said. "Are you sure you don't want to give athletics a rest for a little while?"

"Of course not, I can do it all."

"Well, just as long as you stay on top of your homework."

"There's always so much homework," I complained. "But I can handle it."

I couldn't wait to become a Shadow.

CHAPTER 5

"ARE YOU NERVOUS?" Dad asked as we drove to my first practice with the Shadows.

"Kind of. More excited, I guess."

"Excited about becoming the best basketball team in town?"

"Meeting my new teammates."

"Some of them have only recently moved to town. We're counting on you and Josie to make them feel welcome here," Dad said.

As we walked into the stadium Josie's dad shook Dad's hand, and they walked over to the other parents sitting in the stands. "Good luck, Patty," Dad called.

Josie was standing under the basket at the far end of the court with Uncle Noel and my new teammates. I saw a tall kid there and realized I knew him – it was Luke, a member of our Torres

Strait dance group, Gerib Sik. "Good to see you, *bala*," Luke said. We tapped fists.

Uncle Noel called the group into a circle and said, "Okay, let's go around telling each other a bit about ourselves. Patty, you first."

I smiled at the group. "I'm Patty. My dad is Torres Strait Islander and Mum is Kokatha, from South Australia."

A kid standing across from me said, "That's deadly! I've only met one other fella who is Aboriginal and Torres Strait."

"I played my first season of basketball last year and I love it," I told them. "I'm in the Torres Strait dance group with Josie and Luke and Uncle Noel too."

The really tall and thin fella with skin almost

as black as Dad's said, "I'm Abdi from Somalia. I've just moved to Canberra because Dad's got a new job here with the government."

"And I'm Benny from Brewarrina," said the kid next to Abdi. He had fair skin, was solidly built and had the strongest Australian accent I'd ever heard. "My mob are Ngemba. I haven't played basketball before, but I play league and I'm great at tackling."

We all laughed and Uncle Noel said, "There's no tackling in basketball, Benny. But we can put your other skills to good use."

The kid next to Benny had short black hair, light brown skin and a big, friendly smile. He patted Benny on the back and said, "My name's Bashir and I'm from Afghanistan. My parents came to Australia as refugees, and I go to school with Benny."

I knew Josie was busting to find out more about the next person in the circle.

"I'm Riley," the girl said, and Josie flashed her a big smile. "My family are Ngadjuri from South Australia, and we've been living in Canberra for a couple of years. Mum and Dad are teachers."

Josie and Luke introduced themselves, and when they'd finished Uncle Noel clapped his hands together. "Let's start with a simple drill."

We broke into two groups and took turns dribbling from the halfway line to the basket to shoot.

Benny reminded me of myself when I first started playing. He was trying to run as fast as

29

he could, and slamming the ball into the court when he dribbled. Later, Uncle Noel took him aside and gave him some one-on-one coaching as the rest of us practiced our layups.

WHEN PRACTICE WAS OVER, all the kids and parents got together for a barbecue. The parents couldn't stop talking and laughing, and Benny was telling us stories about where he came from.

"We catch yellowbellies with our hands in Brewarrina," he said.

"What? Yellow-bellied snakes?" Luke asked.

"Nah, what do you think I am,

crazy? Yellowbelly fish, in   the fish traps – all these rocks put there by our ancestors thousands of years ago," he said.

Before we went home, Uncle Noel called the team together. "It was a good session tonight," he said, "but remember that practice doesn't start and end here. If you take some time practicing at home and school, it's amazing how quickly you can improve."

CHAPTER 6

AS WE WALKED to the gym at lunchtime, Josie asked, "Do you think they'll be mad?"

"About what?" I said, but I knew exactly what she was talking about. We were both so excited about playing for the Shadows that we hadn't yet told Coach Clarke, Tyson, Boris, Manu and Tiago that we wouldn't be playing for the same club team as them – the Titans. In fact, we'd be competing against them. Josie gave me a look.

"I just hope they don't feel let down," I said.
"Let's tell them after training. But first let's show
Coach Clarke that we're determined to do our
best for our school team."

We practiced our drills harder and faster than
ever, and when training was over, we waited until
everyone but Coach, Boris, Manu
and Tiago had left the gym.

"Coach Clarke, we want
to speak with you," Josie said.

"What's happening, Josie?"
he asked.

"Patty and I want to play club basketball."

"That's great! We'd love to have you join the
Titans."

I looked at Josie nervously, and she said, "We want to play for a new team that Patty's parents are founding, called the Shadows."

I watched the expression on Coach Clarke's face. But his smile didn't fade at all. "Terrific, the more basketball you play the better!"

Josie and I finally started to breathe again.

AS WE WALKED AWAY, I looked apologetically at my friends. "It's not that we didn't want to join the Titans, guys, but the Shadows is a club for kids from different backgrounds, like us. We really loved the idea of a welcoming space where everyone feels at home."

"It sounds awesome!" Tiago said. "I'd join too if I wasn't already in the Titans!"

Boris punched him playfully on the arm, and we all laughed.

"Thanks for understanding, guys," Josie said, and she shot me a smile.

CHAPTER

7

BEFORE THE FIRST GAME with the Shadows, our families met in the park near the basketball stadium.

Uncle Noel was speaking to some older Aboriginal people, Uncle Jim and Aunty Shirley. They weren't really related to me, but in our culture we address older people as "Uncle" and "Aunty" out of respect for their age and experience.

Uncle Jim and Aunty Shirley were Ngunnawal people; they belong to the Canberra area. I'd seen them at local events, performing the Welcome to Country ceremony, which lets people know whose country they're on, and informs them about the culture and history of the place.

When everyone was gathered, Uncle Noel spoke. "It's with great pleasure that I introduce Uncle Jim and Aunty Shirley to start our jersey presentation."

Uncle Jim stepped forward. "It's great to see you kids here today," he said. "It reminds me of when I was a young fella, and all the friends that I made playing sports."

And then Aunty Shirley said, "It's good to see the new families here with us on Ngunnawal country. We know you've come a long way from your homes in other states and even countries, and we welcome you here to our community."

Uncle Noel handed a jersey to Uncle Jim.

The first person Uncle Noel called up to receive their jersey was Josie. Everyone cheered as she held it up: it was blue with a yellow and white trim, and white numbers. Josie's mum and dad took photos that I knew would be sent straight to her family in the Torres Strait.

When I was handed my jersey I was over the moon to see that I'd be wearing the number eight, the same number my Uncle Danny wore when he played for Australia.

IT WAS AMAZING stepping out onto the court
for the first time with the Shadows, wearing our
brand-new uniforms. Our opposition, the Jets,
wore a blue jersey that didn't look half as flash as
ours.

Abdi was positioned for the tip-off. Aside
from being tall, he could also jump, and he easily

got his hand to the ball and tapped it to Josie. We were off.

Josie was the first to score. I tried to make a couple of layups, but my shots were blocked. It was harder and faster than any of the games I'd played for school.

The big Jets players slapped the ball out of our hands when we were attacking and burst through the key when we were defending. The frustration on Benny's face was clear.

"It's okay, Benny, you're doing well," I told him. But then Benny started pushing the Jets players and bumping them as they drove toward the basket. The referee didn't notice at first, but after the Jets players yelled in protest, Benny got two fouls in under a minute. Uncle Noel had to call a timeout to sub Benny off and settle the team.

For the whole game I only shot one basket, a simple layup. The final score was forty-five to the Jets and twenty-five to the Shadows.

I walked off the court feeling low. I'd never lost at anything by so much. But Uncle Noel said, "You guys did great for your first game together. The score is not an indication of how well you played."

Despite Uncle Noel's encouragement, on the way home I couldn't help thinking again that maybe I just didn't have what it took to be like my Uncle Danny.

CHAPTER 8

"I HEARD YOU GOT WHIPPED by the Jets last night, Patty," Tyson said as we shuffled into class the next day. "You should have joined the Titans. If the Jets beat you by twenty points, you've got no chance against us."

"You said I had no chance of beating you in the four hundred meters," I reminded him. But Tyson had gotten under my skin.

The next time I saw Tiago, I asked him, "Do you guys usually beat the Jets?"

"We won the grand final last year, so, yes. We beat them and everyone else!" Tiago told me.

I gulped, thinking that I couldn't stand to be around Tyson if the Titans thrashed us all year.

AT RECESS I whispered to Josie, "We need to talk."

Josie looked around to see that the others were out of sight. "Is everything all right?"

"Did you know that the Titans won the grand final last year? That means they beat the Jets. And the Jets beat us by twenty points!"

"Patty, it's our first season of club basketball, who cares if every team beats us?"

"I care! I mean, will you be able to stand Tyson paying us out all the time if we keep losing?" I said, raising my hands in the air.

Josie screwed up her face. "You're right, that won't be any fun at all."

"When we play basketball at recess and lunch, let's make sure we join the team with the fewest Titans players on it."

"Why?" Josie asked.

"So we can get used to playing against them, and learn their weaknesses."

TYSON, BORIS, MANU AND TIAGO thrashed us during our game at recess, so I was already agitated going into our math lesson.

Math was my worst subject. At least when it came to literacy, history or geography I knew that if I was stuck, I could study hard to get on top of it. Math was different. I could add and subtract, and I knew all of my times tables, but when it came to fractions, division and multiplication I got confused.

I would listen to Ms. Baker's explanation of the method, but after a while it felt like my head was going to explode. I didn't want to keep asking the teacher for help, so instead I pretended I knew what I was doing. Eventually I wished the ground would open up and swallow me.

Ms. Baker stood in front of the class and said, "Today we're going to start learning long multiplication."

She wrote "183 × 35" on the board and showed us another way to write the problem, explaining that it would help us to solve it, and that the tens and ones of the number needed to be placed in the same columns.

When Ms. Baker started to show us how to work through the problem, I was already lost.

I slumped in my seat. There was no way I'd get through my math homework and tests. And at our school, students need to pass their tests by at least fourteen out of twenty to be able to play sports on Fridays. So there was no way I'd be able to play school basketball again, ever!

CHAPTER 9

I WAS GLAD when dance practice came around. I'd been worrying myself sick about long multiplication, but I knew that as soon as I started dancing I'd stop thinking about it.

Although it was only practice, we all dressed in our traditional costumes. It always made me think of the Torres Strait and my family.

When Uncle Noel started banging his drum,

which we call a *buru buru*, I started to pump my legs up and down.

Uncle Noel stopped. "Listen, Patty," he said. "Listen to the beat. You're going too fast. Dancing isn't about how fast you do the steps, it's not a race. It's about moving with the rhythm."

Uncle Noel started beating the *buru buru* again, and I listened to the beat, letting the sound vibrate through me before I started dancing.

As I began sliding across the floor in time with my group, I imagined the trade winds blowing across the islands, and the waves lapping against the shore. I felt warm inside and that everything was just as it was supposed to be: perfect.

LOOSENING HIS TIE, Uncle Noel called the Shadows together at training. "There are two elements involved in winning basketball: offense and defense," he said. "Tonight we're going to focus on defense."

We did defensive drills, shuffling across the court and side to side. It reminded me a lot of dance practice.

Uncle Noel showed us how to guard a player without fouling when they are driving toward the basket.

At the end of training, Uncle Noel pulled Benny and me aside and said, "Benny, I want you to guard the opposition player bringing the ball down the court. Patty, I want you to be our point guard. Do you know what that means?"

I had a bit of an idea, but listened to Uncle Noel carefully.

"The point guard brings the ball into offense, sets the pace of the game, needs to know all of the plays, and is like the coach on the floor."

I nodded, happy that Uncle Noel was giving me the role, but realizing I didn't know what plays Uncle Noel wanted me to make happen.

"A point guard has to understand the flow and momentum of the game, and I think you have a real talent for that, Patty. But we'll spend a lot of time during the season teaching you how to become a great point guard," Uncle Noel said.

"Cool," I replied. But I wasn't sure if I could do a good job, no matter how much Uncle Noel taught me. What if I always struggled, just like I did with math?

10

BENNY, ABDI, LUKE, AND RILEY were waiting
for us as Josie and I approached the courts on our
bikes on Saturday afternoon.

"What are the teams?" Abdi asked.

"I'm with Josie and Riley," I answered. It
would give Benny an opportunity to practice
his defense against me.

We started, and Abdi teased me with

the ball at first, bouncing it between his legs before running past me and passing the ball to Luke. He did a reverse layup and scored.

"Nice one!" I told him.

The game was intense. We didn't even keep score, we just played as hard and fast as we could.

Benny kept up the pressure on me. Every time I had the ball his tongue hung from his mouth as he concentrated on my every movement, trying to slap the ball away at any opportunity.

After he dribbled his way around Riley, Josie and me to get a well-earned layup, Abdi said, "Let's have a break."

We all walked over to the benches and Riley asked, "What's the time?"

I took my phone from my bag. "Oh man, it's

past four o'clock. We've been playing for almost four hours," I said. "I've got to go." Josie looked at me. She knew I was meant to be at home doing my math homework by now. I felt sick at the thought of it.

Riley wiped sweat from her brow. "Yeah, a replay of the San Antonio Spurs versus Miami Heat game is calling my name."

"A replay of what?" Benny asked.

"You know, the Spurs against the Heat," Riley said, squinting her eyes and tilting her head at Benny.

"I don't know what you're talking about," Benny said, pulling down his cap.

"Haven't you ever watched the NBA?" Luke asked, wide-eyed.

Benny shook his head.

"Well, I'll see you guys. My math homework is calling *my* name," I told everyone.

"Patty, don't worry about your math homework! Weren't you listening? We need to bring Benny up to speed on the NBA!" Riley said.

"I'll help you with your math tomorrow," Josie said.

It didn't take much to convince me. "How about you guys come to my place, then?" I said. "Basketball marathon and sleepover!"

Everyone cheered.

I called my mum and luckily, she agreed.

CHAPTER 11

DAD SET US UP with YouTube on the television, and by quarter time in the replay of the NBA Championship game we'd almost finished our first pizza.

"Why do they keep doing that?" Benny asked.

"Doing what, Benny?" Josie replied.

He described a play that was almost like a choreographed dance, with players moving to

specific parts of the court and passing
to each other in a certain pattern.

"That's called a set play," Dad
said, bringing some drinks in from the kitchen.

"A set play?" I asked.

"Yes, teams will work out moves so that
everyone knows where the ball is being passed
and when a player will be clear to make a shot.
You did well to work it out, Benny."

"But how do they know which routine they're
going to do?"

"Sometimes the coach will tell the team at
the jump ball or time-out," Dad said. "Other
times if the team is finding it hard to score, the
point guard will signal what set play he wants."

"Let's look at that part again," I said.

Before we knew it, we were all on our feet, using a cushion as a basketball, and Dad and Mum were helping us practice the set play we'd just watched.

We ran through the set play about ten times, then watched the rest of the game. We went straight on to another game, then another, until none of us could keep our eyes open any longer.

CHAPTER 12

I WAS FEELING GREAT at school on Monday, but the math lesson after lunch soon put an end to that. I knew there'd be a test the next day.

Again I tried listening carefully to Ms. Baker as she ran through the long multiplication equation on the board.

I scratched my head, looked around the room at everyone working on the calculation in their workbooks, then sank in my seat. I wished I could disappear, or at least fall into a daydream about swimming in the Torres Strait or dunking a basketball. But I was frozen.

Ms. Baker surprised me when she put her hand on my shoulder. "How are you going, Patty?"

I looked up at her and said, "Yeah, all right."

She glanced at my workbook. "You haven't done any work yet?"

"I'm just thinking it through," I told her.

"Well you have a go, and I'll check where you're up to in a few minutes."

I looked at the equation again and started multiplying the numbers on the top of the problem by the ones on the bottom, but I couldn't remember how Ms. Baker carried the tens and hundreds.

When Ms. Baker came toward me I tried to smile cheerfully at her. "It's going fine now," I said, just as another student called her over. As she walked away, Tyson leaned over from the desk in front, eyed my page, and shook his head smugly at me.

THE NEXT MORNING I lay in bed until I heard Mum walk to my door. Then I started groaning. "I feel so sick, Mum."

"What is it?" she asked.

"My head, and my stomach and my chest," I said, coughing.

Mum raised her eyebrows, then went to the

bathroom for a thermometer. She stuck it in my ear and then said, "Your temperature is fine, Patty."

"It must be wrong, Mum. I feel so sick."

She looked at me and narrowed her eyes. "What day is it today?"

"I think it's Tuesday," I answered, snuggling back into the warmth of my bed.

"It's math test day, isn't it, Patty?"

"Yeah, but Mum, I really feel sick."

Mum sighed. "I'm going to send you to school," she said. "If you're still sick at recess I'll leave work and come and get you. But if it's the test that you're worried about, maybe you're spending too much time playing basketball. We might need to rethink all of the training that's cutting into your homework time."

I didn't know how to argue with what Mum had said, so I dragged myself out of bed. "Go to the sick room if you get any worse," she said.

I THOUGHT ABOUT going to the sick room before the test. But I knew I couldn't avoid it forever. I prayed that somehow the answers to the equations would come to me.

I was relieved when I started the test. The first problems were easy: addition and subtraction that I'd learned. But a few questions in, I was hit with a whole lot of long multiplication problems. I decided to give them a go, hoping that Ms. Baker might give me half a mark for trying, or that I might somehow fluke the answer.

MS. BAKER HANDED BACK our tests before recess the next day. I saw Tyson hand his to Boris with a smile spread across his face. Then I looked down at my sheet. It was covered in red pen, and the mark at the top said only seven out of twenty.

Tyson shot to the back of the class to see Nathan and Ben's marks. On his way back to his seat he passed my desk and saw mine. "No wonder you never shoot more than five baskets in a game, Patty. You wouldn't know how to multiply your score." He cracked up.

I tried to act like I didn't care, but there was a hot prickling behind my eyes. I wouldn't let myself cry.

At recess when we were playing basketball, Tyson kept yelling out to me, "What's ten times two, Patty?"

Josie marched up to him. "Will you cut it out, Tyson? He's your teammate."

"He's not my teammate next week. We're playing against the Shadows."

CHAPTER

13

MS. BAKER EMAILED Dad and Mum to tell them about my test results, and they talked to me about it as soon as they arrived home.

"How do you feel about it, Patty?" Mum asked.

"I feel dumb," I replied.

"You're not dumb, bub," she said. "We all come up against things that we find hard to do. But don't worry, math will come to you."

Dad hugged me. "You're one of the smartest people I know, Patty."

Mum put her bag on the counter and switched on the kettle. Then I heard the news I dreaded. "You're going to have to miss basketball on Friday, and maybe you'll have to miss playing with the Shadows tomorrow night to study."

"But that's not fair!" I yelled. "There's only seven of us on the team, and if I don't play there'll be only one sub. It's hard enough playing against teams that have been together forever."

"I understand, Patty. But what's more important, a game of basketball, or improving your math?" Mum raised her eyebrow like she does when she's proving a point.

I didn't answer straightaway. Right now,

basketball felt way more important to me than math ever would be.

"You don't get it," I said, almost crying. "It won't matter how much I study, I'll never understand what Ms. Baker is teaching us. All the other kids get it, why can't I? I'll never be able to play school sports again." I raced to my room and shut the door.

A little while later, Dad and Mum came in. "You can play basketball tomorrow night, Patty," Mum said. I was flooded with relief, but she wasn't finished. "But we will have to meet with Ms. Baker to see what can be worked out for you."

"Come on, Patty," Dad said, rubbing my shoulder. "Come and have dinner. I'm making fish curry, Torres Strait style."

CHAPTER

14

IT WAS A REAL BUZZ walking into the stadium to play my second game for the Shadows.

Riley and Josie were sitting in the stands watching the Titans play against the Jets. The Titans were leading by eight points. I cheered when Tiago made a great steal and passed it to a teammate I didn't recognize at first. Then I realized it was Matthew from St. Michael's. He'd made the difference between St. Mary's and St. Michael's when they beat us in our semifinal last season.

"They're going to be hard to beat," I said to Riley and Josie.

Always positive, Josie said, "Well, we can give it our best shot."

As we warmed up, I looked to our opposition at the other end of the court. The Devils had only one tall player – most of the others were my height. Their shortest player kept taking long practice shots and most of them were going in.

THE FIRST THING we got right playing against the Devils was the tip-off. Abdi tapped it straight to Riley, who passed the ball to me so that we could set up our first shot at a basket.

Playing against the Devils, I started to think that basketball was the most exciting sport ever.

The score was close for the whole game, but the Devils ended up winning by four points. We shook hands with our opposition after the final buzzer, and when we walked off the court our parents came to congratulate us on the great game we'd played.

"I thought I was going to have a heart attack," Abdi's dad said as he ruffled Abdi's hair.

"I've almost lost my voice from cheering so much," said Riley's mum.

"Great game, guys," said Uncle Noel. "I didn't expect such a quick improvement!"

I knew that I'd be doing everything I could to help our team improve even more before we played the Titans the following week.

CHAPTER 15

THE NEXT MORNING we continued our Aboriginal and Torres Strait Islander studies.

Ms. Baker passed some objects around the class. There were some boomerangs, dishes, and another object that looked like a dish but also had a handle.

When it was passed to Tyson, Ms. Baker asked him, "Do you know what you're holding, Tyson?"

His face was blank. I knew he hated not knowing things almost as much as I did.

"It's for scooping water?" Tyson answered.

"Good guess," Ms. Baker said, taking the object from Tyson's hands. She then held it up for us all to see. "This object is called a woomera. There is a place in South Australia called Woomera; it's where rockets are launched. What do you think this woomera is used for?"

Manu shot up his hand, and Ms. Baker nodded in his direction. "It's used to throw spears," he said.

"That certainly is one of its uses, and what it's best known for."

Ms. Baker placed her finger on a point at the end of the woomera and told us, "The end of the spear notches into this point, which is often made of kangaroo bone." She raised the woomera above her head and explained, "The point can be used to reach branches to pick fruit."

"That's cool," Tiago said.

"Can you see the sharp edge on the bottom of the handle? It's quartz, a very hard rock that can be made into a strong cutting tool."

Ms. Baker demonstrated how the woomera could be used to cut. "The quartz is held in place by animal sinew and resin."

Ms. Baker handed the woomera back to Tyson to keep passing around the class. "The woomera can also be used to dig, and as a container for water or food. Some people compare it to a Swiss Army knife. It has many functions."

"It's very light," Darren said.

"What do you think might have contributed to its design?" Ms. Baker asked.

Nobody answered, so she explained. "Many parts of Australia are very hot. The design of the woomera means that the hunter can travel extensive distances with this light object and a spear, preserving energy. The woomera is a lever and demonstrates Aboriginal people's understanding of physics."

Ms. Baker's Aboriginal and Torres Strait Islander studies class made me feel good. It reminded me that my ancestors and my people are very clever.

CHAPTER

16

MY CLASSMATES went and changed into their sports uniforms when the lunch bell rang. I stood on the basketball court by myself and shot free throws.

Everyone poured into the schoolyard wearing their netball, soccer, hockey and basketball gear. I was the only one left wearing my ordinary school uniform.

"Aren't you getting changed, Patty?" Tyson asked as he leapt in front of me and grabbed the rebounding ball.

I shrugged my shoulders and then snatched the ball away from him.

"Oh that's right, you failed the math test, didn't you?" Tyson said, though he clearly hadn't forgotten.

I made another layup and didn't respond.

"Patty can't do math," he teased.

Josie jumped in. "Leave him alone, Tyson," she said. "It means we're one team member down today."

Tyson laughed and walked away.

Before Josie went with the others to the game, I spoke to her. "Let's go and see Uncle Noel after school. We need to get some more tips on how to beat the Titans. There's no way we're going to let Tyson beat us."

"Don't worry, Patty, we'll work things out. For now, just focus on your math."

"Good luck, Josie."

"You too, Patty," she said, giving me a fist tap.

BACK IN CLASS, Ms. Baker sat opposite me. "I met with your parents last night," she said. "They told me how you're feeling about long multiplication."

I nodded, relieved that Ms. Baker finally knew I was having trouble.

"Don't feel bad that you're stuck, Patty. You're

very smart. It will click for you soon, I'm sure."

"You think so?" I asked.

"I know so. How about we start with some problems that you're more familiar with. Let's have a look at some short multiplication."

"Short multiplication?" I asked.

"Yes, short multiplication. You covered it last term, don't you remember?"

"No, I don't know what you're talking about."

Ms. Baker pointed to the equation on the work sheet.

"How's it different to long multiplication?" I asked.

Ms. Baker's eyes suddenly opened wide. "Oh, Patty, you were sick, weren't you? You must have missed the most important lessons on it. No wonder you're having trouble with long multiplication!"

I thought back to the end of last term. I had almost forgotten about the virus that had wiped me out for the last week of school and half the holidays. I'd been stuck in bed for days, boiling hot and achy.

Ms. Baker started to explain short multiplication to me, and at first I thought it would be easy. I knew how to multiply the figure, but I was still finding it hard to see how Ms. Baker was getting to the final answer, even though she was sitting right there with me working through the problem.

I sunk into my chair thinking that I'd never play basketball for St. Mary's ever again.

CHAPTER

17

WHEN JOSIE AND I were sitting at Uncle Noel's kitchen table he asked, "Why do you want to beat the Titans so badly?"

We told Uncle Noel all about Tyson, the things he said about Aboriginal and Torres Strait Islander people, how he teased me about failing my math test, and how he was always giving us a hard time.

Uncle Noel listened carefully, sometimes sucking air through his teeth or screwing up his face when he heard about some of the things that Tyson had done.

When we had finished, he sighed and spoke. "Sometimes people do their best to make others feel miserable because that's how they feel," he said. "If we beat the Titans, it might not make Tyson change his behavior. The most important thing is that you enjoy playing and appreciate improvements when they happen."

"So how can we improve?" I asked.

"Well, it was incredible how much you improved from your first to your second game. How did that happen?"

Josie leaned forward and told him, "We

practiced for hours last Saturday and Sunday, and we ran a set play."

"A set play?" Uncle Noel asked, full of surprise.

"Yeah, Benny noticed that the Spurs were running a set play in a game we watched, so we copied it. You didn't notice?"

"Come to think of it, yes. But I thought it was just you guys repeating something that had worked rather than a set play. You don't usually start learning set plays until you're much more experienced."

"But it wasn't that hard," I said.

"Yeah, we just ran through it about ten times in Patty's lounge room, then practiced it about ten times at the court."

"And how did you all know when to run the

play in the game?"

"When I got past the half-court line I held one finger up," I said.

Uncle Noel smiled. "That's really clever."

"And it worked," Josie said.

"Can we learn some more set plays, Uncle Noel?" I asked.

"We've only got one more training session before the next game," Uncle Noel said, "and we should be focusing on basics."

"The team is getting together tomorrow and Sunday, Uncle Noel. Can we at least try?"

Uncle Noel sat quietly for a moment. "Explain to me the set play you already know."

Josie not only explained the set play,

she drew a diagram of it on a scrap of paper.

"Wait a minute," Uncle Noel said. He walked into another room and returned with two sheets of paper. "Two very simple set plays," he said. "I suggest you give copies of these to your teammates, practice them over the weekend, and we'll see how you're making them work at training. And remember, it's important to feel relaxed about the basics of basketball before you start worrying too much about strategy."

"Excellent, thanks, Uncle Noel," I said, then Josie and I raced home to send copies and instructions to all of the Shadows players.

CHAPTER 18

BY THE TIME WE stepped onto the court to play the Titans we must have practiced our set plays a hundred times. Uncle Noel said we'd perfected them.

Including our original set play, we now had three to choose from. My signals for them were one finger, two fingers or a fist in the air.

We all shook hands before the tip-off. The

Titans were mostly friendly and familiar faces; Tiago and Manu grinned and wished me luck. But as I stood next to Tyson waiting for the referee to toss the ball up, he said, "You're going down."

Boris won the tip-off, but Riley caught the ball. She waited for our players to make their way down to the basket, and then passed me the ball.

Tyson pushed up on me straightaway, but I kept my cool and waited for an opportunity.

I held my fist up in the air, and Abdi ran around me to receive the ball. I screened Tyson. I was watching to see if Luke had started his move toward Abdi, when I felt a huge shove in the back.

The referee blew her whistle, Tyson was called for a foul and I had two shots from the free-throw line.

After I scored the first basket, Tyson spoke to me like I was a baby. "If you get the next one in, Patty, that's two points."

My next free throw didn't go in, but I said to Tyson, "At least that's one more point than you've got, Tyson."

The next moment though, Tyson charged

through our defense and made a layup as if his life depended on it. A few minutes later, the Titans had already scored ten points to our two.

Uncle Noel called a time-out. "You're rushing your shots," he said. "I want you to forget about set plays and just think about passing. I want you to slow the game down and be patient. Wait for the right moment to drive to the basket or take a shot. Does everyone understand?"

We all took Uncle Noel's instructions to heart. Whenever the Shadows had possession of the ball we stayed calm and focused – we didn't rush to the basket but waited – and sure enough, openings began to appear to us. We passed the ball to whoever had the most space, and soon we began to score. By halftime the Titans were only four points ahead.

"Do you want to try another set play after the jump ball?" Uncle Noel asked.

"Why not?" Bashir said, wiping the back of his neck with a towel.

"Don't overdo it, though," Uncle Noel told us. "If it doesn't work, return to the natural flow of the game. If you keep running set plays the opposition and Coach Clarke will catch on."

"Got it," I said.

TYSON GAVE ME a death stare as I took my place by his side for the jump ball. Then we were tussling for best position. The referee looked at us and said, "Watch it, you two."

I stepped away from Tyson, but when the ball was tossed I could feel his hand on my ribs, pushing me aside.

Bashir won the ball. Benny had a clear run to the basket, so he dribbled down the court and looped it over to him. Benny scored.

A minute later, Abdi passed to me. I dribbled casually, looking up to see that everyone was getting into position. I held up two fingers to show my teammates that I wanted to try one

of our plays, and when I was approaching the key and everyone's eyes were focusing on me, we went into action. I was able to make an easy shot.

I could see the panic in

Tyson's eyes when we hit the lead.

Unfortunately, Uncle Noel was right when he said that Coach Clarke would notice if we attempted a play too many times. After the second time, Coach Clarke called a time-out. When we came back onto the court, the Titans' defense was much stronger, with Manu and Tiago jumping into the spaces we wanted to move through.

When the final buzzer sounded, the Titans had it by four points. Tyson wasn't smiling, and I knew he hadn't expected it to be that close. I could tell he was scared of how good we might get by the end of the season.

CHAPTER

19

THE SHADOWS got better and better with each game we played. When we lost, we stayed focused on the areas we had to improve on. We listened to Uncle Noel's instructions and practiced every free moment we had. Before we knew it, we were well into the season, and we'd won several games in a row. We actually had a shot at making it to the finals.

Then Mabo Day came around.

Land is everything to Aboriginal and Torres Strait Islander people, so Mabo Day is a big cause for celebration.

Gerib Sik was performing at Parliament House for the occasion, and I was excited to show off the dance we'd been rehearsing so hard.

I helped members of the dance group get ready as people gathered to watch the performance, including all the students from my school. Uncle Noel was seated on the stage with his *buru buru* and his large seashell. Dad and other uncles, who perform the chanting, sat on the stage with him.

After Uncle Jim and Aunty Shirley welcomed everyone to Ngunnawal country, Uncle Noel blew through his seashell, making a trumpeting sound to start the ceremony. I walked onto the stage bare chested, paying no attention to the cold Canberra morning.

I walked to the center of the stage. "Hello," I said loudly. When I knew the radio mic connected to my head was working I lowered my voice and said, just like I always practiced at rehearsal, "We are Gerib Sik Torres Strait Islander Dance Group, and I am Patty, your Master of Ceremonies. Today, on this special occasion, we will open our performance with the shark dance, from Mer Island in the Torres Strait, the island that Grandad Eddie Mabo is from, the island he fought for."

And then I shot behind the screens at the back of the stage, made sure everyone was ready and then we placed the shark masks, made out of cane, coconut husk and feathers, on our faces and bit down on the piece that made them stay in place.

Uncle Noel started beating the *buru buru* and we got into our positions, our legs pumping up and down to the beat of the drum and the chanting. We held our left arms out straight and our right arms bent at the elbow and to the side, and started to glide like sharks through the reef.

I love the shark dance; performing it makes me feel strong, like a warrior. I left the stage as Josie and the other Torres Strait Island girls walked out to perform, wearing their *augemwali* and *kerim taiir*, floral dresses and headbands.

I watched the girls, thinking back to when Uncle Noel first taught us the shark dance. I was awkward and unsure. But when I took my time and learned the steps, my confidence grew along with my ability.

Just like with basketball. Just like with math.

The Aboriginal and Torres Strait Islander flags waved in the breeze at Parliament House as I went back on stage and started dancing again. I looked out to the audience and saw my teacher and classmates and all of the audience members looking on in amazement.

Then all my thoughts drifted away, and it was just me and my dance group moving as one.

CHAPTER 20

ALL OUR HARD WORK paid off, and by the end of the regular season we had worked our way up into fourth place – which meant we qualified for the finals! We would play the first-place team, the Jets, for a spot in the grand final.

All of the Titans, including Coach Clarke, came to watch us. They had won their semifinal, so whoever made it through this game would be playing them in the grand final. Boris, Manu and Tiago were cheering for us, but when, in a major upset, we defeated the Jets by five points, I could almost feel Tyson's nervous gaze.

Before the start of our next training session Uncle Noel sat us all down in the center of the court.

He took out his large seashell from a backpack and blew it. It boomed through the stadium, the sound bouncing back at us off the walls. He'd never done that at training before. A deep quiet settled over us all.

"When we created the Shadows not long ago," Uncle Noel said, "I didn't imagine that I would be standing here with you only a few months later on the eve of your first grand final. I'm incredibly pleased with what we have achieved – the friendships that I can see developing and how quickly you have all improved your basketball skills."

We grinned happily at each other.

Uncle Noel went on. "Now, I know you're all excited about playing in the grand final. You've done well this season by practicing hard and stretching yourselves, learning advanced strategies like set plays in a big hurry. But, if you want to win this grand final, you need to listen closely to me now. Have you ever heard the expression, 'All good things come to those who wait'?"

"I have," I answered.

"What do you think it means?"

"That if you're patient, you'll

get what you want."

"You're almost there, Patty," Uncle Noel said.

"Maybe it means there's a right time for things to happen," Josie said.

"You've got it, Josie. It's not worth hunting for turtle if it's not turtle season. Our people are very patient people. Before we had all the technology we have today, we had to wait for time and tide and season to get many of the things we wanted. While we waited, we made things like nets and spears for when the time was right to hunt and fish. And even when it was time to hunt and fish, our people still needed to be patient as they waited to throw their spear or cast their net."

Uncle Noel paused for a moment and then asked, "Do you understand what I'm saying?"

Benny said, "I reckon you're trying to tell us not to rush in the game. To wait for the best passing and shooting options."

"That's exactly what I'm saying," Uncle Noel said with a warm smile. "Our two previous games against the Titans have been very close. I believe the way to beat them is to take your time, take control of the game, make things happen when they need to happen," he said. "Come on, let's get into it."

WHEN I WALKED INTO the stadium with my teammates for the grand final, it was the most nervous I'd ever been before a game, or even a test. The stands were the fullest I'd seen them.

We all sat with our parents and watched the last minutes of a younger team's final. The winning team were jumping up and down and hugging each other. The kids on the losing side looked miserable. I remembered how I had felt when our school team lost the semifinal against St. Michael's. I tried not to think about it, took a deep breath, and focused on how my body felt, strong and full of energy.

I shook Tyson's hand when we walked onto the court. "Good luck," was all I said to him. He didn't respond. I shook hands with Boris, Manu and Tiago, and they all smiled at me and wished me luck. It was strange going up against my close friends. But I knew they understood I had to do my best.

By the time I was standing at the jump ball, the only thing on my mind was getting my hands on the ball. Then, when the referee tossed the ball up, Tyson pushed me straight into Tiago. The referee didn't see Tyson push me, only me crashing into Tiago, and a foul was called against me. Tiago shot me a knowing look when the ball was passed to him, and his team ran down to their end of the court. I was angry, but I knew that was what Tyson wanted. I tried to calm down, telling myself that there was still a whole game ahead of us.

Tiago dribbled down the court and passed to Boris, who dashed out past the three-point line and shot before Abdi could push up on him. The ball bounced off the backboard and went in. The Titans supporters went wild.

"It's okay, we've got this," I told Abdi as he took the ball to pass it back in.

Abdi ran ahead of me as I brought the ball down. I passed to Luke, who passed to Benny, close to the key. The Titans players crowded around Benny, and he crouched down and made a bounce pass between their legs out to Bashir, who had time to shoot and score two.

We all patted Benny on the back for his smart assist.

"Don't give him an inch, Benny," I said just before the ball was passed in to Tyson.

IN THE FIRST HALF the Titans kept up their forceful attack, but the Shadows kept our nerve, and when the halftime buzzer went, we were leading by two points.

As we were leaving the court, Tyson hurled the ball at me when I wasn't looking. It smacked me right in the guts and knocked the wind out of me.

I was gasping for air, and Uncle Noel came and helped me over to the bench. "Are you all right, Patty?"

I tried to tell him that I was all right, but I couldn't catch my breath. Josie put her hand on my shoulder and looked at me with a concerned expression. Dad came down from the stands and handed me a bottle of water. "Stand up straight, Patty. Try to suck some air in," he said.

Finally I caught my breath and was able to speak. "I'm okay," I said.

"I'm going to talk to the referee," Uncle Noel said with a deep frown.

"It's okay, Uncle Noel," I told him. "I'll sort it out."

WE SAT ON THE BENCH, drinking water, catching our breath and cooling down. I knew everyone was worried about me – they kept checking that I was okay. Then I laughed and said, "We're winning," and everyone else laughed too.

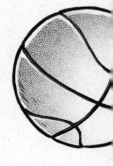

Uncle Noel smiled and said, "Yes, we are winning – but let's not get ahead of ourselves. Patience, remember?"

I DIDN'T WANT TO give anything away to Tyson. So when we stepped back on the court for the second half, I looked him in the eye as if nothing had happened.

I received the ball from Abdi and dribbled toward the basket. When I made the shot, Tyson gave me a massive shove. I heard an angry murmur from the crowd – some people must have seen his earlier behavior toward me too. This time, the referee called the foul against Tyson.

"Come on, Patty," I heard people calling out from the stands as I moved to the free-throw line.

I bounced the ball twice, concentrated on the hoop, then took a shot. It swished through the net. Our supporters went crazy, but I told myself not to get caught up in the excitement. I had to focus on the next shot.

Again I went through my routine. As soon as I pushed up through my legs and the ball rolled off my fingers, I knew I was going to make the next free throw. *Swish* went the ball as it dropped through the net.

Tyson took off recklessly, and Benny was right on him. When Tyson turned and bounced the ball I stole it, and dashed to the basket to score another two points.

I knew we'd rattled the Titans, and my excitement seemed to give me even more energy.

When I was bringing the ball down the court I saw Uncle Noel holding his hand out in front of him, telling me to steady things down. I looked around. All the Shadows were in their positions, and I held up one finger, telling them I wanted us to run our set play.

It ran like clockwork, with quick passes from me to Benny to Josie, who scored us another two points, putting us up by eight.

"We've got them now," Josie said. But within seconds, Matthew scored a three-pointer. Then Tiago stole the ball from Luke when we were attacking, and the Titans scored another three points.

Now we were only leading by two. I felt a wave of nervousness sweep over me as I looked up at the time clock and saw that there were only two minutes remaining in the game.

I dribbled the ball back down the court. Riley, Josie, Abdi and Luke were all racing around the key with their arms stretched above their heads. I passed to Riley, and she dribbled away from the basket, turned and shot. The ball bounced off the hoop and straight to Boris. Matthew and Tyson were already making a fast break down the court.

Boris hurled the ball to Matthew, and it felt like a replay of the losing semifinal I'd played in against his school team. Matthew pulled up outside the three-point line. The ball bounced off the backboard and straight through the hoop.

Now they were leading by one.

The Titans fans went crazy. Tyson jumped all over Matthew as if they'd won the game.

Uncle Noel called a time-out.

"I know there's less than a minute left, and it probably feels like you need to race to the basket – but believe me, you don't. It's really the time to be patient. Remember what we talked about?"

We all nodded, trying to catch our breath.

"It's all about being patient until the best opportunity to score opens up," Uncle Noel went on. "Have you got it?"

"Yes," we all said, and Uncle Noel sent us back out.

I dribbled the ball down the court as fast as I could, but once I hit our attacking zone I slowed down. I thought about how I had been rushing my steps at dance practice. It was time to move with the rhythm of the game.

I passed the ball to Josie. She dribbled the ball away from the basket and passed to Riley. Riley held the ball above her head and passed to Abdi. I was watching from outside the three-point line and thought that Abdi was going to drive to the basket and make a layup. But he paused, then passed the ball out to me. There were four seconds left on the clock.

I could hear everyone yelling, "Shoot it, Patty!"

I took a jump shot.

Tyson was right in front of me defending, and I couldn't see if the ball had gone in. But

when all my teammates started jumping over me, I knew it had. The roar from the stands erupted at the same moment as the buzzer sounded. I looked up to see Uncle Noel with his arms raised above his head.

CHAPTER

21

I COULDN'T WIPE THE GRIN off my face for days after the grand final. My mum and dad both said how proud they were – not just that we had won, but that I had kept a cool head and done my best for the team in the face of Tyson's cruel comments and bullying behavior.

I was thinking about their words when I sat down for my math test.

As I sat there looking at the more difficult long multiplication equations, I pictured Uncle Noel saying, "All good things come to those who wait – be patient." I tried looking at the equation differently, taking my time, moving through the steps I needed to solve it. And then, all of a sudden, it made sense. I didn't need to see Ms. Baker's tick to know that I'd solved it correctly.

OUR BASKETBALL ASSOCIATION held an awards dinner, and everyone brought dishes to share. The parents of my team-mates brought some of their traditional foods. Riley's parents brought some

kangaroo kebabs. Dad made his delicious curry crab, and Josie's mum made a coconut curry fish.

When we were standing at the table dishing up our food, Tyson sidled in next to Riley and me.

"Want to try some kangaroo kebabs?" Riley asked him. "They're my favorite."

"Of course," he answered.

I looked at him in surprise. "Really?" I said. "It's bush tucker, you know."

"Yeah, I know. I've had it before."

"When did you try it?" I asked.

"Reconciliation Week. This food is delicious," he said, piling up his plate. "And Patty, I was a real jerk, hey?"

I looked at Tyson, noticing that I'd grown at least another inch taller than him. I could have easily agreed. But he looked me in the eye, a meek, embarrassed smile on his face. "You're all right, *bala*," I said. "Try some of Dad's curry crab."

GLOSSARY

Aborigines: Aboriginal. People indigenous to Australia.

athletics park: stadium or place for practicing and competing in athletics (skills like running, jumping, and throwing. Commonly called track and field).

athletics: skills like running, jumping, and throwing. Commonly referred to as track and field.

bala: brother. Language of Torres Strait Islander people.

buru buru: island drum. Language of Torres Strait Islander people.

bush tucker: plants and animals traditionally taken from the land and the sea and cooked in special ways by Aboriginal and Torres Strait Islander people.

cricket: a game played with a hard ball and flat bat on an oval grass field. It started in England.

dugong: a medium-sized mammal that lives in the ocean.

footy: short for football. "Footy" means the game of Australian Rules (Aussie rules) football and the ball itself. The ball and the field are oval shaped.

g'day: good day; a greeting.

give [something] a go: take a chance; give it a try.

goody-goody: a term given to someone who is acting well-behaved.

half a mark: half credit.

have a go: take a chance; give it a try.

holidays: vacation.

home straight: home stretch.

How are you going?: How's it going? How are you doing?

league: rugby league, a game similar to American football.

literacy: reading and writing.

lollies: candy.

lounge room: living room.

Mabo Day: a day to remember Eddie Mabo and Australia's High Court legal decision that recognized traditional laws and customs and the rights Meriam people have to their island of Mer (Murray) and its waters of the Torres Straits.

milk bar: a general store or cafe.

netball: a game like basketball that is played with a ball similar to a soccer ball.

paying us out: making fun of us.

put [something] down to: credited [something] to.

quarter time: the break at each quarter in a game like basketball.

Reconciliation Week: an annual celebration of Aboriginal and Torres Strait Islander peoples' history, cultures and achievements. A remembrance of the 1967 referendum when Australians voted to have Indigenous people included on the national census.

sick room: a room at school for people who are sick; nurse's room or office.

steady things down: slow things down.

Torres Strait: the waters and group of islands between Australia and Papua New Guinea, the traditional home of Torres Strait Islander people. Australia has two Indigenous groups, Aboriginal and Torres Strait Islander.

Torres Strait Islander: Torres Strait Islander people, Indigenous to Australia.

Welcome to Country ceremony: an event where Aboriginal and Torres Strait Islander traditional owners welcome others to the land of their ancestors. It shows respect for traditional owners and elders of particular areas or regions.

witchetty grubs: a traditional Aboriginal bush tucker food. The grubs (moth larvae) are found in the woody roots of certain bushes and are a rich source of protein for Aboriginal people living in remote areas of Australia.

woomera: spear thrower, a traditional wooden tool used by Aboriginal men when hunting for food. A spear attached to the sharp end of the woomera travels much faster and farther, and can be thrown with great accuracy.

you lot: referring to a group or gathering of people.

PATTY MILLS was born in Canberra. His father is from the Torres Strait Islands, and his mother is originally from the Kokatha people in South Australia. Patty plays with the San Antonio Spurs in the NBA and is a triple Olympian with the Australian Boomers (Beijing '08, London '12, Rio de Janeiro '16).

JARED THOMAS is a Nukunu person of the Southern Flinders Ranges. His novels include *Dallas Davis, the Scientist and the City Kids* for children, and *Sweet Guy, Calypso Summer* and *Songs that Sound Like Blood* for young adults. Jared's writing explores the power of belonging and culture.